Library of Congress Cataloging-in-Publication Data

Scarry, Richard.
  Richard Scarry's favorite storybook ever / Richard Scarry.
      p. cm.
  "A Golden Book."
  "This book originally published in slightly different form in *Funniest
Storybook Ever* by Random House, Inc., in 1972 and 1982, and in *What Do
People Do All Day?* by Random House, Inc., in 1968 and 1979."
  Summary: A collection of sixteen stories featuring the animals of
Busytown.
   ISBN 0-375-82549-5
   1. Children's stories, American. [1. Animals—Fiction. 2. Short
stories.] I. Title: Favorite storybook ever. II. Title.
   PZ7.S327 Fav 2003
   [E]—dc21
                                    2002152708

Richard Scarry's
Favorite Storybook Ever

A GOLDEN BOOK • NEW YORK

www.goldenbooks.com

ISBN: 0-375-82549-5

PRINTED IN CHINA

10 9 8

The Talking Bread

Humperdink, the baker, was mixing bread dough with the help of Able Baker Charlie Mouse. His little girl, Flossie, watched them squish and squash the dough.

After they had kneaded the dough by squishing and squashing, they patted it into loaves of all different shapes and sizes.

Then Humperdink put the uncooked loaves of bread into the hot oven to bake.

After the loaves had finished baking,
Humperdink set them out on the table to cool.
Mmmmm! Fresh bread smells good!

Mamma!

Finally he took out the last loaf.
LISTEN! Did you hear that?
When he picked up that loaf, it
said, "Mamma." But everybody knows
that bread can't talk.
  IT MUST BE HAUNTED!!!

Humperdink picked up Flossie and ran from the
room.
  "I must telephone Sergeant Murphy," he said.

Sergeant Murphy arrived in a hurry.

He reached down and picked up
the loaf of haunted bread.

Mamma!

"Mamma!" the bread said.

Murphy was so startled he
fell into the mixing trough.

At just that moment, Huckle
and Lowly came into the bakery.

"That is a *very* strange loaf of bread," said Lowly.
He stretched out and slowly ooched across the floor to it.

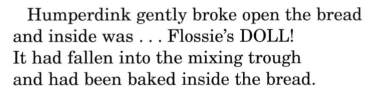

He took a nibble.
The bread said nothing.

He nibbled and nibbled until only his foot was showing . . . and still the bread said nothing.

Mamma!

Lowly stood up.
The bread said, "Mamma!"

Lowly took another nibble, then stuck out his head.
"I have solved the mystery," he said. "Break the loaf open very gently, but *please* . . . don't break me!"

Humperdink gently broke open the bread and inside was . . . Flossie's DOLL! It had fallen into the mixing trough and had been baked inside the bread.

With the mystery solved, they all sat down to eat the haunted bread. All of them, that is, except Lowly. He had already eaten his fill.

All right, Lowly! Please take your foot off the table!

9

The Three Fishermen

Lowly, Huckle, and Daddy were going fishing.

Their little motorboat took them far away from shore.

Daddy said, "Throw out the anchor, Lowly."
Lowly threw out the anchor . . . and himself with it!

Lowly climbed back in and Daddy began to fish.

Daddy caught an old bicycle.
But he didn't want an old bicycle.
He wanted a fish.

10

Then Huckle fell overboard.
Wouldn't you know that something
like that would happen?

Daddy pulled Huckle back into the boat.
Why, look there! Huckle caught a fish in his pants!

Daddy fished some more, but he
couldn't catch anything.
   He was disgusted.
   "Let's go home," he said. "There
just aren't any fish down there."

As Daddy was getting out of the boat,
he slipped . . . and fell!
   Oh, boy! Is he ever mad now!

But why is he yelling so loudly?

11

Aha! I see!
A fish is biting his tail.
The fish is trying to catch Daddy!
It is good that Daddy has a strong tail.
Now Lowly is the only one who hasn't caught—

Wow!

But look! Lowly has taken off his hat.
Do you see what is under it? A FISH!
Very good, Lowly.

Yes, there you see three
very good fishermen!

Mr. Fixit

Mr. Fixit can fix ANYTHING.
At least, that is what he once told me.

He fixed the wheel on Philip's wagon.

He fixed Mrs. Pussycat's automobile.

He fixed Sam's boat so that
it wouldn't ever leak again.
My, that was a leaky boat!

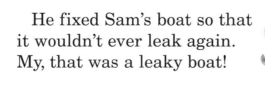

He fixed the flat tire
on the school bus.
Don't you think you
should stop now, Mr. Fixit?

He also fixed a broken streetlamp.
What's the matter with Doctor Bones?
Can't he see where he's going?

Dadda!

Mary's talking doll couldn't
say "Mamma" anymore.
Mr. Fixit fixed it.
Now it says "Dadda."

He fixed Mother Cat's
vacuum cleaner, but he made a
little mistake. It won't vacuum
the floor anymore—only the
ceiling!
    Mr. Fixit told her she was
lucky to be the only one with
a vacuum cleaner like that!

He fixed Lowly Worm's shoe.
"You are a genius," said Lowly.
"I'll bet there isn't anything
you can't fix."
"You are right, Lowly," said
Mr. Fixit. "I can fix anything."

Then Mr. Fixit went home for supper.
After his wife kissed him, she said,
"Will you please give Little Fixit
his bottle while I am fixing supper?"
Mr. Fixit filled the baby bottle
with milk. BUT . . . he didn't know
how to fix the nipple on the top.

He tried and he tried, but he couldn't
get it on. What a mess he was making!

Little Fixit said, "Daddy, let me try."
"It can't be done," said Mr. Fixit.
But he let Little Fixit try anyhow.
And Little Fixit fixed it—
on the very first try!

"WHY, THAT'S AMAZING!" said Mr. Fixit.
"Show *me* how to do it."
Now, just be patient, Mr. Fixit.
Let him finish his bottle first,
and *then* he will show you how.

Special Delivery

Betsy Bear wrote a letter to Grandma to wish her a happy birthday.

She went to the post office to mail it.

She bought an airmail stamp and stuck it on the envelope.

She put the letter in the letter slot.

The postmen stamp all the letters with an inked postmark stamp.

The ink postmark tells you the name of the town the letter was mailed from. The address shows where the letter is to go.

From Betsy Bear Busytown

To Grandma Bear West Street Workville

Uncle Benny, the postmaster, read the address on each letter. All the neighboring towns have cubbyholes in Busytown Post Office. Uncle Benny put all the letters that were going to Grandma's town in one cubbyhole. He put the letters going to other towns in different cubbyholes.

Then he put all the letters that were going to Grandma's town in a mailbag.

He took the mailbag to Busytown Airport and put it on an airplane.

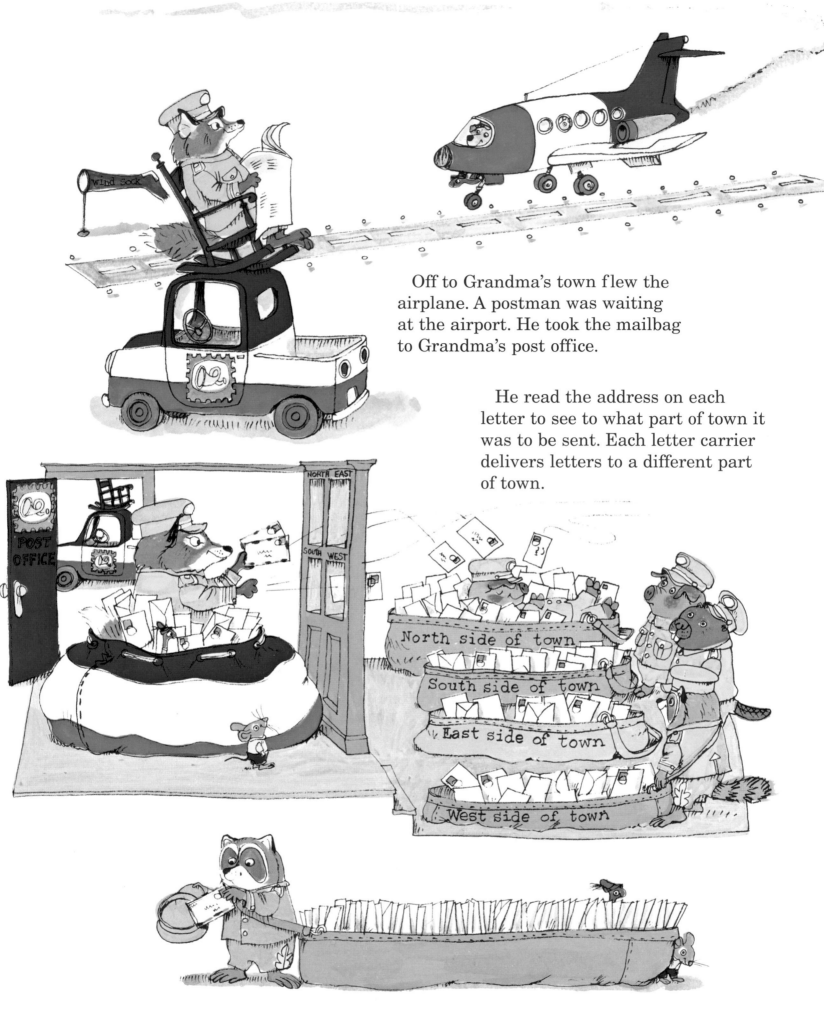

Off to Grandma's town flew the airplane. A postman was waiting at the airport. He took the mailbag to Grandma's post office.

He read the address on each letter to see to what part of town it was to be sent. Each letter carrier delivers letters to a different part of town.

North side of town

South side of town

East side of town

West side of town

Soon the bag of Zip, the letter carrier, was stuffed full. There was no more room for the last letter, so he put it in his hat.

STOP! STOP!
Where is my birthday letter?

Sorry, Grandma!

Grandma was waiting for a birthday letter from Betsy.

But Zip walked right past her house! He said he didn't have a letter for Grandma in his bag.

She asked him to please look again. So he did.

No! Sorry! No letter for Grandma. He tipped his hat good-bye—and a letter fell out! It was Betsy's letter to Grandma!

"Why, Zip! You dear postman!" she said. "You DID bring me a letter from my granddaughter after all!"

She was so happy that she gave Zip a big kiss. Grandmothers just LOVE to get letters from their grandchildren!

Happy Birthday
Grandma
Love and
Kisses xxx
Betsy

Tanglefoot

Tanglefoot was going to the supermarket to buy a can of soup for his mother. She told him to be careful not to trip or fall.

"I never trip or fall," said Tanglefoot.

1 one   He tripped and fell out the front door.

2 two   He tumbled over a baby carriage.

3 three   He then fell into the supermarket.

4 four   He bumped into the grocer.

5 five   He knocked over the butcher.

6
six He tripped . . . and cans of soup went flying all over.

7
seven *Ooof!* Big Hilda was in his way.

"I must stop tripping and falling," he said to himself.

8
eight But then he fell over the checkout counter.

He walked home without tripping once. Very good, Tanglefoot! He even helped his mother make a big pot of soup for supper.

But when she poured it into a big bowl, he fell into it!
Tanglefoot said, "I don't think I can trip and fall anymore today."

9
nine

10
ten But he did!

Good night, Tanglefoot. Sleep tight.

A Visit to the Hospital

Mommy took Abby to visit Doctor Lion.
He looked at her tonsils.
"Hmmmm. Very bad tonsils," he said.
"I shall have to take them out.
Meet me at the hospital tomorrow."

The next day, Daddy drove them to the hospital.
Abby waved to the ambulance driver.
Ambulances bring people to hospitals
if they need to get there in a hurry.

Nurse Nelly was waiting for Abby.
Mommy had to go home, but she
promised to bring Abby a present
after the doctor had taken her
tonsils out.

Nurse Nelly took Abby up to the children's room.

Roger Dog was in the bed next to hers.
His tonsils were already out.
He was eating a big dish of ice cream.

Nurse Nelly put Abby on the bed.
She pulled a curtain around them.
No one could see what was going on.

Why, she was helping
Abby put on a nightgown!

Doctor Lion peeked into the room.
He told Nurse Nelly he was going
to put on his operating clothes.
He told Nurse Nelly to bring
Abby to the operating room.

Off to the operating room they went.
Doctor Lion was waiting there.
Everyone but the patient wears
a face mask in the operating room
so that germs won't get spread.

Doctor Lion told Abby that she
was going to go to sleep.
He said she would stay asleep
until her tonsils were out.

Doctor Dog held a mask
over her nose and mouth.
Abby breathed in and out.
In an instant she was asleep.

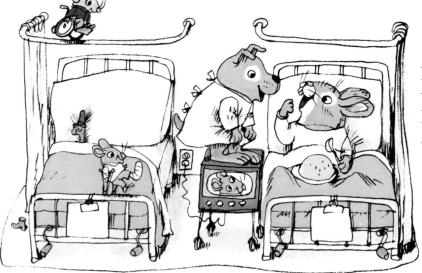

When she woke up she found
herself back in the bed next
to Roger's. Her tonsils were all gone!
Her throat was sore, but it felt better
after she had some ice cream.

Whooooeeee!
Abby saw her mommy arriving
in the ambulance. Abby thought
her mother must be in a hurry to
see her.

Hurry!

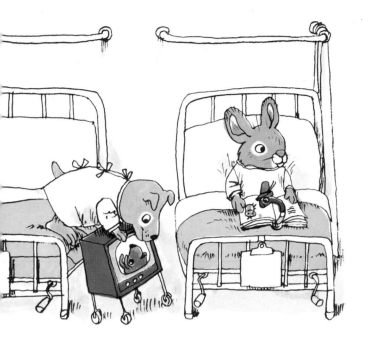

Abby waited and waited—
but Mommy didn't come.
At last Doctor Lion came.
"Your mother has brought
you a present," he said.
He took Abby for a ride
in a wheelchair.

"There is your present," he said.
"It is your new baby brother! Your
mother just gave birth to him here
in the hospital."
Then they went to Mommy's
room in the hospital.
Daddy was there, too.

What a lucky girl she was!
She left her tonsils at the
hospital, but she brought
home a cute baby brother.

He looks like me, don't you think?

But remember! Very few children receive such
a nice present when they have their tonsils out!

Sergeant Murphy and the Banana Thief

Sergeant Murphy was busy putting parking tickets on cars when suddenly, who should come running out of the market but Bananas Gorilla. He had stolen a bunch of bananas and was trying to escape.

Murphy! LOOK! He is stealing your motorcycle, too!

Sergeant Murphy was furious.

Huckle and Lowly Worm were watching. Huckle said, "You may borrow my tricycle to chase him if you want to."

B-r-e-e-e-t!

Away they went . . . chasing that naughty thief.

They raced through the crowded street.
Don't YOU ever ride your tricycle in the street!

They crossed a drawbridge just as it
was opening to let a boat go through.

27

Bananas stopped suddenly and went into a restaurant.

Murphy said to Louie, who was the owner,
"I am looking for a thief!"
Together they searched the whole restaurant,
but they couldn't find Bananas anywhere.
Louie then said, "Sit down and relax, Murphy.
I will bring you and your friends something delicious to eat."

Somebody had better pick up those banana peels
before someone slips on one. Don't you think so?

Louie brought them a bowl of banana soup. Lowly said, "I'll bet Bananas Gorilla would like to be here right now."

"Huckle, we mustn't forget to wash our hands before eating," said Sergeant Murphy. So they walked back to the washroom. Lowly went along, too.

When they came back, they discovered that their table had disappeared.

Indeed, it was slowly creeping away . . . when it slipped on a banana peel. And guess who was hiding underneath.

Sergeant Murphy, we are very proud of you!
Bananas must be punished. Someday he has to learn that it is naughty to steal things that belong to others.

Building a New Road

Good roads are very important to all of us.
Doctors need them to visit patients.
Firemen need them to go to fires.
We all need them to visit one another.

The road between Busytown and Workville
was bumpy and crooked and very dusty . . .

. . . except when it rained!
Then the dirt turned to mud and everyone got stuck.

The mayors of the two towns went to the road engineer
and told him that they wanted to have a new road.
The townspeople had agreed to pay the road engineer
and his workers to build the new road.

Get rid of those bumps!
Make this road flat and straight, Bugdozer!

surveying instrument

BUMP

ROAD PLANS

OK, chief!

The surveyor used his instruments to make sure the road would be straight.

The **grader** makes the **ground smooth**

The **motor crane** lifts heavy things

The road builders used many machines to build roads. They put down big pipes to let streams of water flow under the road.

The **bulldozer** moves **dirt**

The surveyor's helpers used stakes and string to show where the road was to go.

water drainage ditch

tractor shovel

ditch digger

dump truck

At last the roadbed was straight and smooth. But it needed a hard top so that there would be no dust or mud.

Big rocks were put into the rock crusher
to be crushed into smaller stones.

A stone spreader spread the stones
evenly over the roadbed.

A truck squirted sticky asphalt oil
on the stones to make them stick together.

The stonecutter shaped
the stones so that they
would fit next to each other.

The asphalt mixer made hot, sticky asphalt.

The asphalt was poured into
the level finisher, which spread
it out flat on the road.

A heavy roller
pressed down the asphalt
to make it hard and smooth.

A GOOD ROAD

How am I
doing, chief?

The road was built high in the middle
so that rainwater would roll off into
ditches at the sides.

35

Streetlights were put up so that drivers could see the road clearly at night.

FIREFLY LIGHTING COMPANY

electric cable

SNACK BAR

EAT

GASOLINE

gas pump

gasoline storage tank

GAS AND OIL

OIL OIL OIL OIL OIL OIL

DIVIDING LINE PAINTER

GARDENER

All right, you two fellows! Stop talking and finish covering up that underground gasoline storage tank!

The workers put up guardrails
to keep cars from going off the road.

They posted many signs.
Some signs remind drivers to drive safely.
Some signs show which way to go.

A dividing line painter painted a line down the middle of the road.
Dividing lines remind drivers to keep on their own side.

Don't push!

Everyone wanted to be first to
drive on the new road. But
Grandma Cat was the first!
Wasn't she lucky?

37

The Unlucky Day

Mr. Raccoon opened his eyes.
"Wake up, Mamma," he said.
"It looks like a good day."

He turned on the water.
The faucet broke off.
"Call Mr. Fixit, Mamma," he said.

He sat down to breakfast.
He burned his toast.
Mrs. Raccoon burned his bacon.

Mrs. Raccoon told him to bring
home food for supper.
As he was leaving, the
door fell off its hinges.

Driving down the road,
Mr. Raccoon had a flat tire.

While he was fixing it,
his pants ripped.

38

He started off again.
His car motor exploded
and wouldn't go any farther.

He decided to walk.
The wind blew his hat away.
Bye-bye, hat!

While chasing after his hat, he fell into a manhole.

Then he climbed out and bumped into a lamppost.

A policeman yelled at him for bending the lamppost.

"I must be more careful," thought Mr. Raccoon. "This is turning into a bad day."

He didn't look where he was going. He bumped into Mrs. Rabbit and broke all her eggs.

Another policeman gave him a ticket for littering the sidewalk.

His friend Warty Wart Hog came up behind him and patted him hard on the back. Warty! Don't pat so hard!

"Come," said Warty. "Let's go to a restaurant for lunch."

Warty ate and ate and ate.
Have you ever seen such bad
table manners?
 Take off your hat, Warty!

Warty finished and left without
paying for what he had eaten.
Mr. Raccoon had to pay for it.
Just look at all the plates
Warty used!

The lunch cost Mr. Raccoon
every penny he had with him.
 "What other bad things can
happen to me today?" he wondered.

Well . . . for one thing, the tablecloth could catch on his belt buckle!

"Don't you ever come in here again!"
the waiter shouted.
"I had better get home as quickly as
possible," thought Mr. Raccoon. "I don't
want to get into any more trouble."

He arrived home just as Mr. Fixit was leaving.
Mr. Fixit had spent the entire day finding new leaks.
"I will come back tomorrow to fix the leaks," said Mr. Fixit.

Mrs. Raccoon asked her husband if he had brought home
the food she asked for. She wanted to cook something hot
for supper. Of course, Mr. Raccoon hadn't, so they had
to eat cold pickles for supper.

After supper they went upstairs to bed.
"There isn't another unlucky thing that
can happen to me today," said Mr. Raccoon
as he got into bed.
Oh, dear! His bed broke! I do hope that
Mr. Raccoon will have a better day
tomorrow, don't you?

41

Speedboat Spike

Speedboat Spike liked to take his little boy, Swifty, out for a ride in his speedboat. Oh, my! Didn't Spike think he was smart!

Once he rammed into a sailboat.

Say! Why don't you look where you're going?

Another time he bumped into a barge and knocked a lady's laundry overboard.

Swifty! Why don't you tell your father to stop being such a dangerous driver?

42

Speedboat Spike just wouldn't slow down,
and he wouldn't stop bumping into things.

But that was before Officer Barnacle caught him . . . and made him stop!

Officer Barnacle ordered Speedboat Spike to keep
his speedboat in a wading pool UP ON LAND!
Now Spike can go as fast as he likes,
but he won't be able to bump into anyone.

But who is that I see
in that tiny little speedboat?
Why, it's his boy, Swifty!
Oh, dear! I think we are going to need
another wading pool.
Go get him, Officer Barnacle!

Set Sail

Captain Salty and his crew are getting their ship ready for a voyage. The ship will carry passengers to visit their friends in a faraway land across the ocean.

At last the ship is loaded with
the food and other things they
will need on the long trip.
Here come the passengers!

They have all bought tickets
for the trip. They give the tickets to the
purser before they can go aboard. NO PUSHING, PLEASE!

light buoy

Tooooooooot!
It is sailing time. A tiny tugboat pushes
the big ocean liner away from the pier.
Bon voyage! The big ship sails out of the harbor.

45

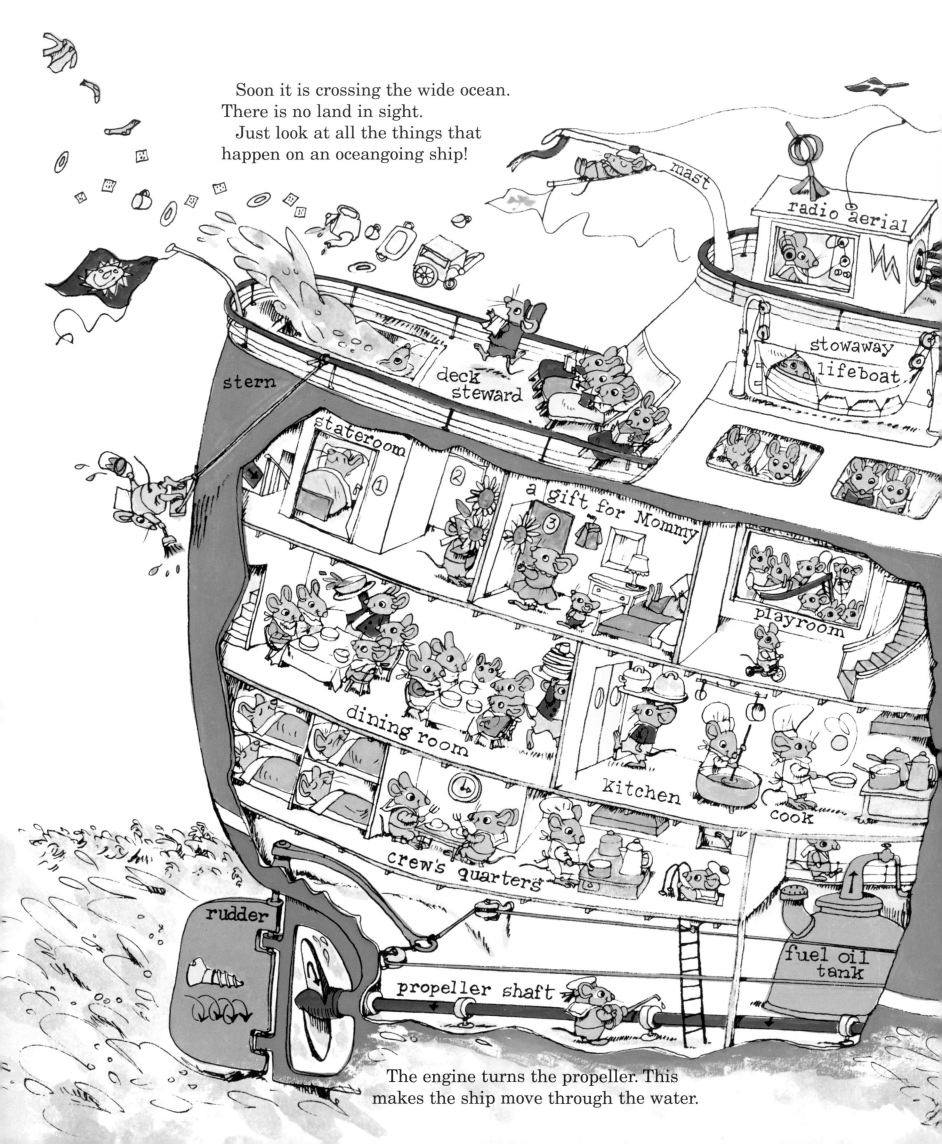

Soon it is crossing the wide ocean.
There is no land in sight.
Just look at all the things that
happen on an oceangoing ship!

mast

radio aerial

stowaway lifeboat

stern

deck steward

stateroom

1

2

a gift for Mommy

3

playroom

dining room

kitchen

cook

crew's quarters

rudder

propeller shaft

fuel oil tank

The engine turns the propeller. This
makes the ship move through the water.

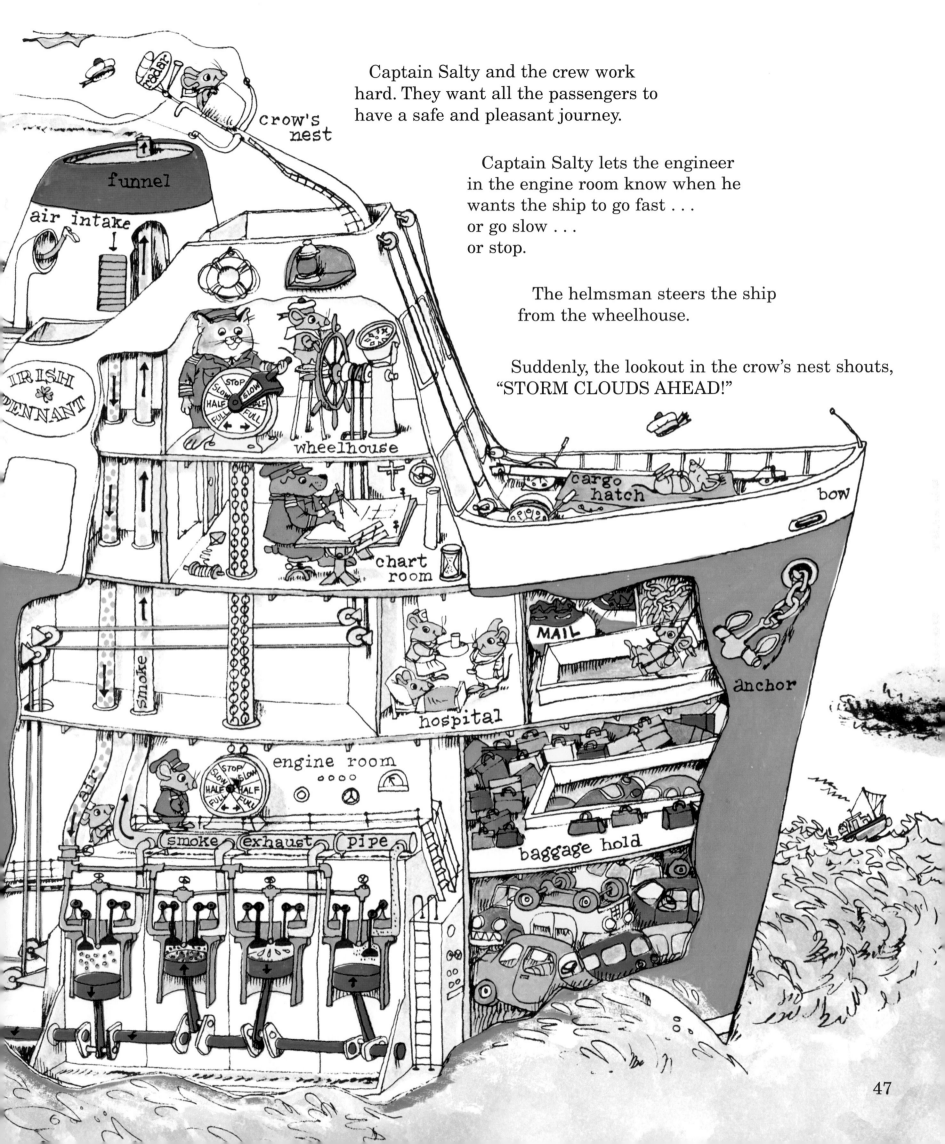

Captain Salty and the crew work hard. They want all the passengers to have a safe and pleasant journey.

Captain Salty lets the engineer in the engine room know when he wants the ship to go fast . . . or go slow . . . or stop.

The helmsman steers the ship from the wheelhouse.

Suddenly, the lookout in the crow's nest shouts, "STORM CLOUDS AHEAD!"

crow's nest

funnel

air intake

IRISH PENNANT

wheelhouse

chart room

cargo hatch

bow

smoke

hospital

MAIL

anchor

air

engine room

smoke exhaust pipe

baggage hold

The storm hits the ship with great fury! The radio operator hears someone calling on the radio.
"SOS! HELP! SAVE US! OUR BOAT IS SINKING!"

Look! There it is!
It's a small fishing boat in trouble!

"FULL SPEED AHEAD!"
roars Captain Salty.
My, the sea is rough!

"LOWER THE LIFEBOAT!"
Hurry! Hurry! The fishing boat is sinking!
Sailors Miff and Mo row to the rescue.

The boat sinks, but the fishermen are safe.

It's delicious!

LAND HO!!!

Back on board the liner, Captain Salty
gives a party to celebrate the rescue.
Will the storm never stop?

Then, just as suddenly as it started,
the storm is over and the sea is calm.
The ship continues on its journey.

Land ho! They have reached
the other side of the ocean!

Everyone thanks the captain and crew for such
an exciting voyage. Then they go ashore to visit friends.
Other people have been waiting to cross the ocean
to visit friends in Busytown. I wonder if their
voyage will be as exciting as this one was?

The Three Sitters

Mother Bear saw Wolfgang, Benny, and Harry
walking by. She ran out and said, "My house
is a mess. I've got to clean it from top to
bottom. Will you please baby-sit Robert
while I go shopping for some soap?"

Wolfgang, Benny, and Harry all agreed to stay
and play with Robert while Mother Bear was shopping.

After a while they got tired of playing.
   "I have a good idea," said Harry. "Let's make
some fudge."
   I don't think Mother Bear would approve of that,
do you?

When they had finished
mixing everything together,
they poured it into a pan.
Do you suppose they *really*
know how to make fudge?

Then they all sat down at the kitchen
table to wait for the fudge to cook.
Gurgle, burble! Burble, gurgle!
Something seems to be bubbling over!

POP!!!!
The oven door burst open.
The fudge had exploded!
RUN!

Lowly ran to the telephone.
"HELP!" he cried. "The fudge is rising!
Our house is sinking in fudge!"

Look out, everyone! Here come the firefighters now.
My, they are quick.

But Lowly, WAIT!
Don't turn on the hydrant until the
firefighters attach the big hose to it.

Soon every bit of fudge had been washed
out of the house . . . along with a few other things.
   But LOOK! Who is that coming?
Why, it's Mother Bear. Hurry up, fellows!
Straighten the house before she gets home.
Put everything back in place.
   And hurry up they did!

"I have never seen my house looking so spic
and span," said Mother Bear. "I think we should
have a party. Who would like to make some fudge?"
   Lowly spoke right up. "I think it would be
better if you made it, Mother Bear."
   And so she did. And everyone ate the best fudge
in the cleanest, spic-est and span-est house ever!

Absentminded Mr. Rabbit

Mr. Rabbit walked down the street. He wasn't looking at the workmen, who were making a new, hot, sticky, gooey street. No! He was looking at his newspaper.

He wasn't looking at his feet, which were getting hot and sticky and gooey, too. No! He was looking at his newspaper.

Then suddenly he stopped looking at his newspaper. He looked down at his feet instead. And do you know what he saw? He saw that he was STUCK in that hot, sticky, gooey street!

The workmen got a long pole and tried
to poke him out. It didn't work.

A truck tried to pull him out with a rope.
No good! He was stuck, all right!

They tried to blow him out with a huge fan.
The fan blew off his hat and coat . . .
but Mr. Rabbit remained stuck.

Some firefighters tried to squirt him out.
They squirted water at his shirt and necktie . . .
but Mr. Rabbit remained stuck. REALLY STUCK!
Well, now! He can't stay that way forever!
Somebody has to think of a way to get him out.

Aha! Here comes a power shovel!
Let's see what it will try to do.

Well, the power shovel reached down . . .
and scooped up Mr. Rabbit.

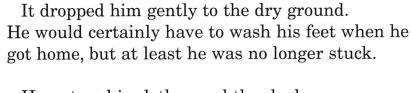

It dropped him gently to the dry ground.
He would certainly have to wash his feet when he
got home, but at least he was no longer stuck.

He put on his clothes and thanked everyone.
As he was leaving, he promised that after this
he would always look where he was going.

But a little while later he was reading his newspaper again, and he had forgotten his promise. Naturally, he wasn't watching where he was going.

OH!!! DON'T LOOK!!!

The New House

Huckle lived with Mommy and Daddy in a part of Busytown where there were no other houses nearby. There were no other children to play with. Huckle was very lonely.

Then one day a man came and dug a hole in the empty lot next door. Someone was going to build a new house. Huckle wondered if there would be any children in the new family.

58

Jason, the mason, made a foundation in the hole for the house to be built on. His helper mixed cement to hold the bricks together.

Sawdust, the carpenter, and his helpers started to build the frame of the house. Jason started to build a chimney.

I wonder if any children will live there?

Jake, the plumber, attached the water and sewer pipes to the main pipes under the street.

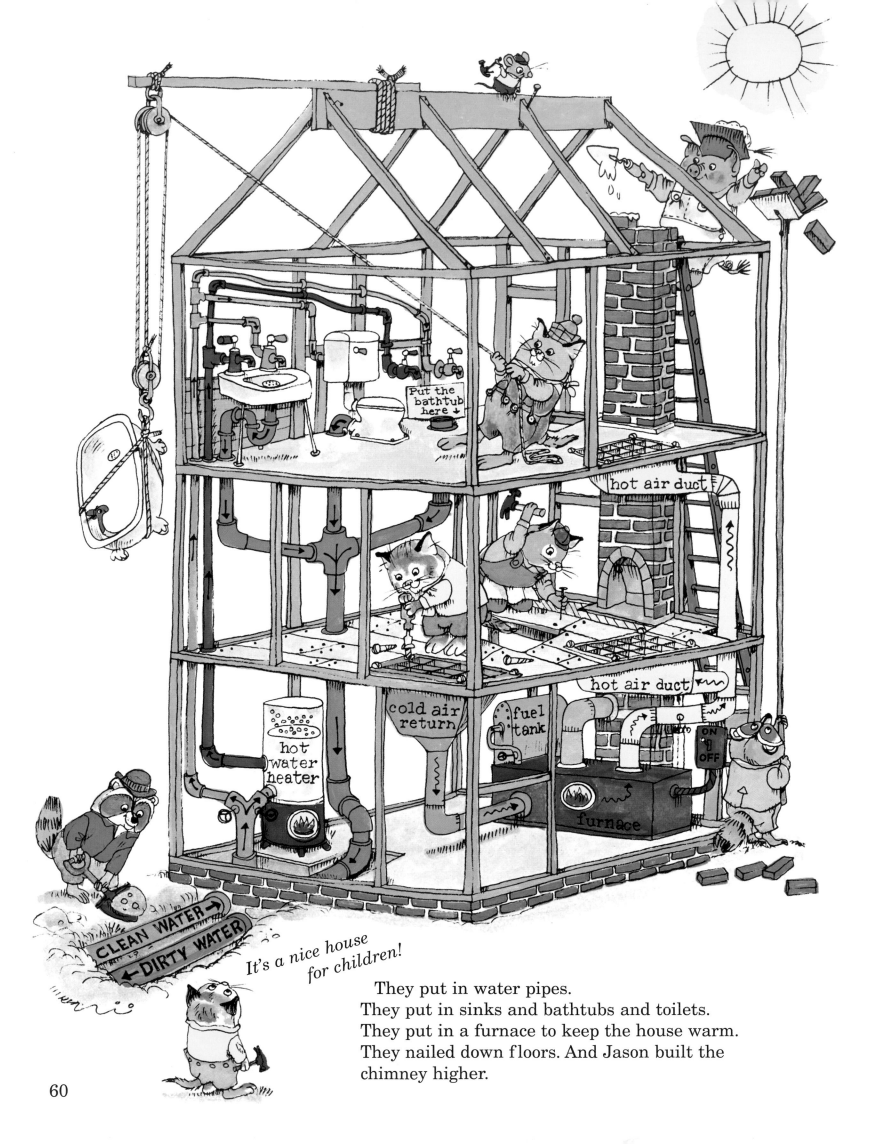

CLEAN WATER →

← DIRTY WATER

Put the bathtub here ↓

hot air duct

hot air duct

cold air return

fuel tank

hot water heater

furnace

ON OFF

It's a nice house for children!

They put in water pipes.
They put in sinks and bathtubs and toilets.
They put in a furnace to keep the house warm.
They nailed down floors. And Jason built the chimney higher.

60

Jason finished making the chimney.
Be careful you don't fall, Jason!

electricity and telephone utility pole

fuse box

NEVER, NEVER
TOUCH!

They put a roof and sides on the house. The
electrician put in electric wires. All kinds of
telephones were put in.

61

The electrician attached electric switches and outlets to the wires.

Sawdust nailed up the inside walls. The walls covered up all the pipes and wires.

He put windows where they belonged—and doors, too.

The house was painted inside and outside.

stove

refrigerator

sink

clothes washer

A truck brought furniture, a television set, a radio, rugs, pictures, a stove, and lots of other things. The house was ready for the new family.

At last the new family has arrived! Look! It is Stitches, the tailor! Stitches paid the workmen for building the house.

bag of money

And here is Stitches' family.
"Look, children," said Mother Stitches.
"We have found a new playmate for you."
And Huckle was never lonesome after that.

The Accident

Harvey Pig was driving down the street.
Better keep your eyes on the road, Harvey.

Well! He didn't keep his eyes on the road,
and he had an accident.

Breeet!

Sergeant Murphy came riding along.
"Everyone get on the sidewalk," he said.
"I don't want anyone arguing in the street.
You might get run over."
So everyone got on the sidewalk.

And just in time, too!
Rocky was driving his bulldozer down the street.
"I'm very sorry about that," he said. "I guess
I wasn't looking where I was going."

All right, now. Keep calm, everybody!
Here comes Greasy George, the garage mechanic.

Greasy George towed away the cars, and the motorcycle, and all those loose pieces.
"I will fix everything just like new," he said. "Come and get them in about a week."

65

Greasy George worked and worked to make everything just like new again.

Stand back, Lowly and Huckle! Don't get too close to him!

Well! Greasy George was certainly telling the truth. When everyone came back, everything was certainly NEW!

I don't know how you did it, Greasy George, but I think you got the parts a little bit mixed up!

My cap!

Calling Sergeant Murphy! Your little girl, Bridget, won't take her nap. Hurry home immediately.

Ma Pig's New Car

Pa Pig bought a new car to give
to Ma Pig on her birthday.
    She will certainly be surprised
when she sees her new car, won't she?

On the way home, Pa stopped at a drugstore.
When he came out, he got into a jeep by mistake.
    You should be wearing your glasses, Pa Pig!
Harry and Sally thought that Pa had swapped cars with a soldier.

Stop, thief!

Then he went to the supermarket.
When he came out, he got into a police car.
    "You made a good swap, Daddy," said Harry.
    But Pa wasn't listening . . . and he didn't seem to be
thinking very well, either. Don't you agree?

67

Next he drove to a fruit stand to buy some apples.
When he left, he took Farmer Fox's tractor.
My, but Pa is absentminded, isn't he?
"Ma will certainly like her new tractor," said Sally to Harry.

They stopped to watch a fire. When the fire was
out, they left . . . in the fire engine!
How can *anyone* make so many mistakes?

Hey, Joe! You forgot to turn off the motor.

Then they stopped to watch some workers who were
digging a big hole in the ground.
No! Pa did NOT get into that dump truck.
But by mistake, he got into . . .

. . . Roger Rhino's power shovel!
  Ma Pig was certainly surprised to see her new CAR!
But Pa! Do you know how to stop it?

Yes, he did!
  Uh-oh! Here comes Roger now.
He has found Ma Pig's new car
and is bringing it to her.
  It looks as though he is very angry
with that someone who took his power shovel.

ROGER! PLEASE BE CAREFUL! You are squeezing
Ma's little car just a little bit too tightly.
  Well, let's hope that Pa Pig will never
again make *that* many mistakes in one day!